W9-CCT-247

LAUREN CHILD is one of the top children's author-illustrators in the UK. Her Charlie and Lola series of picture books have been made into a BBC television series. Her other title for Frances Lincoln is *Dan's Angel*.

Lauren was inspired to write *I Want a Pet* after watching her friend look longingly in pet shop windows. Lauren once had sixteen guinea pigs, two goldfish, two hamsters, one tortoise and hundreds of stick insects!

**For my mother and father who gave me my first pet Michael (a goldfish)
and ended up with 16 guinea pigs, 2 hamsters and a tortoise**

I want a Pet copyright © Frances Lincoln Limited 1999
Text and illustrations copyright © Lauren Child 1999
The right of Lauren Child to be identified as the author and illustrator of this work has
been asserted by her in accordance with the Copyright, Designs and Patents Act, 1988
(United Kingdom).

First published in Great Britain in 1999 by
Frances Lincoln Children's Books, 4 Torriano Mews,
Torriano Avenue, London NW5 2RZ
www.franceslincoln.com

This edition first published in the USA in 2011.

All rights reserved

No part of this publication may be reproduced, stored in a retrieval
system, or transmitted, in any form, or by any means, electrical,
mechanical, photocopying, recording or otherwise without
the prior written permission of the publisher or a licence
permitting restricted copying. In the United Kingdom
such licences are issued by the Copyright Licensing Agency,
Saffron House, 6-10 Kirby Street, London EC1N 8TS.

A catalogue record for this book is available from
the British Library.

ISBN 978-1-84780-289-7

Set in Stone Sans

Printed in Dongguan, Guangdong, China by Kwong Fat Offset Printing in July 2011

1 3 5 7 9 8 6 4 2

I Want a Pet

Lauren Child

F

FRANCES LINCOLN

CHILDREN'S BOOKS

I *really* want a pet.

   "Please Mom, can I have a pet?"
   Mom says, "Well – perhaps something
with not too much fur."
   Dad says, "Maybe something that lives outside."
   Grandma says, "Nothing with a buzz."
It interferes with her hearing aid.
   Grandad says, "Stuffed pets are very reliable."

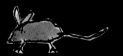

The pet shop lady says, "Goldfish can be fun."

I say, "How?"

Mom asks, "What sort of pet would you like?"
    I say, "How about an African lion? I'd train him
and we could do a show. We'd be a roaring success."

Grandma says, "Lions have a habit of snacking between meals."

I think uh-oh.

"A sheep would be nice, and they're vegetarian.
We could knit sweaters together."

Grandad says, "Sheep are forever following you around. They haven't got minds of their own."

I hate copy-cats.

"How about a wolf? I bet they have lots of good ideas. And wolves are good sniffers, so we'd never get lost."

Dad says, "Wolves are also good at howling.
Howling gives me a headache."

Dad isn't much fun when he's got a headache.

"Maybe an octopus is the answer. They're quiet, and we could go diving in the bath."

Mom says, "Have you any idea how many footprints an octopus would make?"
I say, "Eight."

Mom says, "Exactly."

"A boa constrictor would be perfect. They don't have legs, and they hardly make a sound."

Dad says, "Boa constrictors have a habit of wrapping themselves around you and squeezing too tightly."

Maybe I want a pet that's a bit less friendly.

"How about a bat? At night we could flap around, and during the day we'd dangle upside-down in the closet."

Mom says, "If anyone mentions bats in the closet, there'll be no chocolate éclairs!"

Chocolate éclairs are my favorite

So I must try and find a pet that
won't eat me,
won't copy my ideas,
won't make too much noise,

won't leave dirty footprints round the house,
won't squeeze me too hard,
and won't make my mom so cross she cancels
chocolate éclairs.

The pet shop lady says she can think of one thing that doesn't leave footprints, doesn't eat, doesn't move and doesn't make a squeak.

No one's exactly sure what it is, because it's not quite a pet yet . . .

but it will be soon.

MORE TITLES FROM
FRANCES LINCOLN CHILDREN'S BOOKS

BATTY
Sarah Dyer

No one notices Batty hanging upside down at the zoo.
But trying to join in with the penguins, the gorillas and
the lions is not for him. It's only when he returns to the
bat enclosure that he makes a surprising discovery about
what he is really good at.

Turn the book around to see Batty's upside down point
of view, in this funny and original story by an exciting
and award-winning picture book talent.

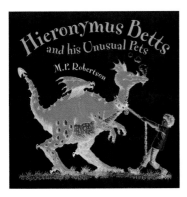

Hieronymus Betts and his Unusual Pets
M.P. Robertson

Hieronymus Betts has some very unusual pets.
But he knows of something that is slimier, noisier,
greedier, scarier, and stranger than all of them
put together. But what on earth could it be?
Dare you read this book to find out?

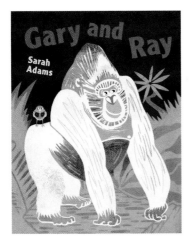

Gary and Ray
Sarah Adams

Gary the gorilla is the only animal in the jungle who
is lonely – even the people of the village are frightened
of him so stay well away. But one day a tiny sunbird thinks
he looks so sad that he ventures to talk to him. Soon this
unlikely pair are best of friends. But then one day Ray
doesn't show up and Gary is even more bereft.

Frances Lincoln titles are available from all good bookshops.
You can also buy books and find out more about your favorite titles,
authors and illustrators on our website: www.franceslincoln.com